MATCH WITS WITH
SHERLOCK HOLMES
Volume 6

MATCH WITS
WITH
SHERLOCK HOLMES

The Adventure of the Abbey Grange

The Boscombe Valley Mystery

adapted by
MURRAY SHAW
from the original stories by Sir Arthur Conan Doyle

illustrated by **GEORGE OVERLIE**

 Carolrhoda Books, Inc./Minneapolis

To young mystery lovers everywhere

The author gratefully acknowledges permission granted by Dame Jean Conan Doyle to use the Sherlock Holmes characters and stories created by Sir Arthur Conan Doyle.

Text copyright © 1991 by Murray Shaw.
Illustrations copyright © 1991 by Carolrhoda Books, Inc.
Series Editor: Marybeth Lorbiecki

This book is available in two editions:
Library binding by Carolrhoda Books, Inc.
Soft cover by First Avenue Editions
241 First Avenue North
Minneapolis, MN 55401

Library of Congress Cataloging-in-Publication Data

Shaw, Murray.
   [Adventure of the Abbey Grange]
   The Adventure of the Abbey Grange ; The Boscombe Valley Mystery / adapted by Murray Shaw from the original stories by Sir Arthur Conan Doyle ; illustrated by George Overlie.
      p.   cm. — (Match Wits with Sherlock Holmes : v. 6)
   Summary: Presents two Sherlock Holmes adventures, each accompanied by a section identifying the clues mentioned in the story and explaining the reasoning used by Holmes to find a solution. Includes a map highlighting the sites of the mysteries.
   ISBN 0-87614-666-3 (lib. bdg.)
   ISBN 0-87614-550-0 (pbk.)
   1. Dectective and mystery stories, American. 2. Detective and mystery stories, English—Adaptations. 3. Children's stories, American. 4. Children's stories, English—Adaptations. [1. Mystery and detective stories. 2. Short stories. 3. Literary recreations.] I. Doyle, Arthur Conan, Sir, 1859-1930. II. Overlie, George, ill. III. Shaw, Murray. Boscombe Valley Mystery. 1991. IV. Title. V. Title: Adventure of the Abbey Grange. VI. Title: Boscombe Valley Mystery. VII. Series: Shaw, Murray. Match Wits with Sherlock Holmes ; v. 6.
PZ7.S53425Ab   1991
[Fic]—dc20   91-15901
                                                                                        CIP
                                                                                        AC

Manufactured in the United States of America

1 2 3 4 5 6 7 8 9 10 00 99 98 97 96 95 94 93 92 91

CONTENTS

In the year 1887, Sir Arthur Conan Doyle created two characters who captured the imagination of mystery lovers around the world. They were Sherlock Holmes—the world's greatest fictional detective—and his devoted companion, Dr. John H. Watson. These characters have never grown old. For over a hundred years, they have delighted readers of all ages.

In the Sherlock Holmes stories, the time is always the late 1800s and the setting, Victorian England. Holmes and Watson live in London, on the second floor of 221 Baker Street. When Holmes travels through back alleys and down gaslit streets to solve crimes, Watson is often at his side. After Holmes's cases are complete, Watson records them. These are the stories of their adventures.

INTRODUCTION

Over the course of Watson's friendship with Holmes, Watson marries and moves to new lodgings. On occasion, though, he still stops by Baker Street to check on his friend. Holmes is as quick as ever to use his detective skills on Watson. The doctor recalls:

As usual, Holmes's greeting was not hearty, but he seemed glad to see me. "Watson," he said, offering me my old armchair, "wedlock seems to suit you. You've put on at least seven and a half pounds since I last saw you."

"Seven," I answered.

"A trifle more, I fancy. And I see you have been trudging out in the wet and have a clumsy maid."

"Holmes," I said, amazed, "had you lived a few centuries ago, you would surely have been burned for being a witch. I did come back from a walk in the country a dreadful mess. But I have since changed my clothes. And I let our maid Jane go because she was unsuitable. But how did you know?"

"It is simple, indeed," Holmes replied. "My eyes tell me that the inside of your left boot has six parallel cuts. This happened, no doubt, when a careless maid tried to scrape mud from your boot. Thus, two deductions from one observation—the careless maid and the wet weather."

"When I hear your reasons, Holmes, these things always appear ridiculously simple. Yet, until you explain them, they remain a mystery. Even so, I'm sure my eyes are as good as yours."

"Certainly, my good Watson. But you see and don't observe. For instance, you have frequently used the steps which lead to our rooms."

"Quite frequently."

"And how many are there?"

"Why, I'm not sure."

"That is precisely my point. You have seen but have not observed. There are exactly seventeen steps. I both saw the steps and took note of what I saw. And that is the lesson to be learned."

It was a lesson I learned over and over.

*"Finally, to my astonishment, he climbed
up on the enormous oak mantelpiece."*

THE ADVENTURE OF
THE ABBEY GRANGE

One bitterly cold morning in '97, I was awakened by a tugging at my shoulder. There, holding a candle in his hand, was Holmes. His tense, excited look told me something was amiss.

"Come, Watson, come!" he cried. "The game is afoot! Not a word. Into your clothes and come!"

Ten minutes later, we were in a cab, dashing through the dark, icy streets to Charing Cross Station. We arrived just in time to catch a train to Kent. Once we had some hot tea to thaw us out, Holmes began to speak and I to listen.

He drew a note from his pocket and read:

> *The Abbey Grange*
> *Marsham, Kent*
> *3:30 a.m.*
>
> *My dear Mr. Holmes,*
> *I should be very glad of your immediate assistance, for this promises to be a most remarkable case. Except for letting the lady go, everything shall stay as it was found. I beg you not to lose an instant! It is difficult to leave Sir Eustace there.*
> *Yours faithfully,*
> *Stanley Hopkins*

"Each time Inspector Hopkins of Scotland Yard has sent for me," Holmes remarked, "the case has turned out to be memorable. And I note with pleasure, Watson, that his cases have all found their way into your collection. However, I must object to the bad habit you have of writing everything as a story. Each case should be a demonstration of the scientific method! You may excite your readers, but you fail to instruct them."

"Then perhaps you should write them yourself," I returned, with some bitterness.

"I will, my dear Watson, I will," Holmes stated smugly, blowing at his tea. "Someday I shall write a textbook on the art of detection. At the present, however, I am quite busy. It seems our newest demonstration is one on murder."

"You think Sir Eustace Brackenstall is dead?"

"Quite," said Holmes matter-of-factly. "Hopkins is not an emotional man, and his note shows signs of great mental disturbance. Yes, I gather there has been some violence. The body must have been left where it lay. According to my calculations, the crime had to have been committed before midnight."

"How can you possibly tell?" I asked, astonished.

"It's quite simple. The local police had to investigate and then call in Scotland Yard. Inspector Hopkins must have taken a night train to Kent, took a look at the scene, and then wired for me. All that makes a fair night's work."

Holmes smiled and settled back to ponder the details of the murder. I nestled sleepily into my seat to await our arrival. Just after dawn, our train reached Chisle-hurst Station. A frosty drive over narrow country lanes brought us to the wrought-iron gates of the Abbey Grange. Inside, an avenue of ancient elms led to the aged abbey. The grand old home had stately pillars and was shrouded in leafless ivy.

Inspector Hopkins awaited us at the door. His young face was fresh and eager. "I'm glad you have come, Mr. Holmes. And you, too, Dr. Watson! But I should not have troubled you. The lady has just given us the full story of what happened, and very little is left to be done. Do you remember that Lewisham gang of burglars?"

"What, the three Randalls?" I asked.

"Exactly," said Hopkins, "the father and two sons.

It's their work, no doubt. They did a job at a village nearby only a fortnight ago. Sighted and then described in the paper, they were. Rather cool of them to do another job so soon. But this time, it's definitely a hanging matter."

"Sir Brackenstall is dead, I presume," said Holmes.

"Yes, indeed," chattered Hopkins. "He had his head knocked in with a fireplace poker. And his wife seemed half-dead when I first saw her. I suggest you hear her story before you examine the dining room."

The lady in question was a woman of singular beauty. Seldom have I seen so graceful a figure, so womanly a presence, so lovely a face. Golden hair and blue eyes complemented a perfect complexion.

Lady Brackenstall was lying on the morning-room couch in a blue-and-silver dressing gown. Beside her lay a black sequined dinner dress. Though she could hardly be twenty-years old, she looked pale and tired. A hideous plum-colored swelling over her eye marked her delicate features. A tall, stern woman was bathing the young woman's forehead with vinegar and water.

"Mr. Hopkins, I have told you all that happened," Lady Brackenstall moaned. "Must I repeat the horrible affair?" She shuddered and buried her head in her hands. As she did, the sleeves of her loose gown fell back from her wrists.

"You have other injuries, madam!" cried Holmes. "What are these?" Two red spots stood out vividly on her white arm. She covered them hastily. "They have nothing to do with last night's horrible events. If you and your friend sit down, I will tell you all I can."

We did as she asked, and the weary mistress began to speak. "Sir Eustace Brackenstall and I have been married only a year. Still, there's no use trying to hide the fact that our marriage has not been a happy one. I grew up in South Australia, where I lived as I pleased. This life in England—with all its proper manners—has not suited me in the least. Worst of all, Sir Eustace is, or was, an utter brute, and all the villagers know it." The woman's eyes blazed with anger. But the tall servant's gentle hand soothed her, and the lady began to sob passionately.

At last, she continued, "You may know that in this house, all the family's rooms are in this old section. All the servants sleep in the modern wing. Theresa, my maid, is the only servant in this wing. Last night, Sir Eustace went to bed about half-past ten. I stayed up reading in the library. At around eleven, I went, as usual, to see that everything was locked up. When I came to the dining room, I felt a strong draft. So I pulled the drapes aside to shut the tall French window. Suddenly I found myself facing an elderly, broadshouldered man. Two younger men stood behind him in the garden."

Lady Brackenstall sat up. "I stepped back, but the old fellow was on me in an instant. I tried to scream, but he hit me in the forehead. I must have fallen unconscious. When I came to, I was tied to a chair by the bell rope. My mouth was bound tightly with a handkerchief, and I could not move.

"Just then, my husband burst into the room, grasping his favorite blackthorn walking stick. Two of the men rushed at him, and the eldest hit him in the head with the fireplace poker. My husband fell without a sound. I must have fainted then."

Lady Brackenstall paused. "The next thing I remember is seeing the thieves taking our silver from the cabinet. The old man boasted that he would have some of our fine wine before he left. He poured each of them a glass. The younger men toasted the old man. I gathered that they were a father and two sons. They drank their wine, and after what seemed like ages, they turned to check on me. I quickly closed my eyes and tried not to move. Finally they left. I struggled for a while and managed to get my mouth free to scream. Theresa came running. She alerted the rest of the household and called the police." The young widow took a deep breath. "There now . . . that is all. I trust that I shall not be forced to go over so painful a story again."

Hopkins turned to Holmes, who had been listening patiently. "Any more questions, Mr. Holmes?" the inspector asked.

"No," said he, shaking his head. "I would not wish to tire you further, Lady Brackenstall. I would, however, like to hear your maid's story."

The older woman stiffened, growing inches taller. "I quiver to think of it now," she began. "Last night, from my bedroom window, I saw three men in the moonlight down by the gate. I thought nothing of it at the time. Later I heard my poor lamb scream. Down I ran to find her just as she says, and him on the floor, with blood all over. It was more than a mind can bear! Now you've put my dear through enough. Old Theresa here is taking her to her room to get the rest she needs." With motherly tenderness, the maid helped Lady Brackenstall out of the room.

"Theresa Wright has been with the lady all her life," said Hopkins. "You don't find maids like her nowadays. She nursed Lady Brackenstall as a babe and came over with her from Australia."

Holmes did not seem to be listening. His interest in the case seemed to have passed. He followed Hopkins to the dining room with an air of impatience. But as he entered the room, the strange scene that met him fanned his dying interest.

The chamber was very large, with a high, carved-oak ceiling. Hunting trophies decorated the wood walls. At the end of the room was the tall French window Lady Brackenstall had described. Three smaller windows threw light onto a heavy oak chair near the fireplace. Woven through the chair's cross-pieces was a crimson bell rope. The maid must have slipped the rope off Lady Brackenstall when she released her—for the rope was still knotted. We noticed all these details later, for our eyes went at once to the man who lay dead on the tigerskin rug.

Sir Eustace was staring up at us fiendishly—his white teeth clenched with hatred through his short, black beard. An embroidered nightshirt covered his trousers, and his feet were bare. His head was horribly injured. Over the man's enormous shoulder was flung the hand holding the walking stick. Beside him rested the heavy, bent poker that had killed him.

"This thief must have been an extremely powerful old man," said Holmes.

"Yes," agreed Hopkins. "The Randalls are known to be pretty rough customers. What beats me is why they left Lady Brackenstall alive."

"Exactly," said Holmes. "They knew she could identify them."

"They may not have realized," I suggested, "that she had recovered from her faint."

"That seems likely enough," said Holmes. He bent over the chair to look closely at the sailor's knots and the frayed edges of the red bellpull. Then his eyes lit up. "If they pulled at the bell rope, it must have rung in the kitchen. How could they take such a chance?"

"Indeed, Mr. Holmes," said Hopkins. "The thieves must have known the habits of this house well. They counted on the fact that the kitchen bell would be difficult to hear at night, since most of the servants sleep in the other wing. Perhaps the thieves worked with one of the servants—but they all seem loyal."

"What type of man was Sir Eustace?" I asked.

"When he was sober," Hopkins answered, "he was charming, good-hearted, and kind. But he became a regular fiend when he drank. Once, he shot his wife's dog, and another time, he threw a bottle at her maid."

"That would make the maid a possible suspect,"

Holmes noted to himself. "Yet," he added, "it seems very unlikely that Miss Wright would have betrayed her mistress."

Holmes walked to the French window and threw it open. He bent over the lawn below. "There are no footprints," he called. "The ground is too hard." My friend straightened up to give the room one last look. "What did the thieves take?"

"Some silver," Hopkins replied. "The lady thinks the men were so disturbed by the murder that they decided not to search the rest of the house."

"No doubt that is true. But then why did they take the time to drink a glass of wine?" Holmes said dryly.

"To steady their nerves?" Hopkins proposed.

"I'm sure they needed it. Halloa! Halloa! What have we here?" Holmes's expression had suddenly changed to razor-edged alertness as he examined the dusty, half-filled wine bottle on the side table. Three glasses were grouped near the bottle. All of the glasses were tinged with wine, and one had some wine dregs in the bottom.

"Remarkable!" cried Holmes. "Is Lady Brackenstall sure she saw all the men drinking?"

"Yes," said Hopkins. "What can you possibly find remarkable about that?"

"Why did they not finish the bottle? And, well, let it pass. It must be due to mere chance," my companion said, shrugging. "Perhaps when a man has special knowledge and special powers like mine, he looks for a complex explanation when a simple one is at hand.

Certainly the lady's story rings true. There is no more for me to do. Keep me posted, Inspector. I would enjoy hearing the Randalls' story once they are caught." Holmes reached for his coat and hat. "Come, Watson, I fancy we may employ ourselves better at home."

———— ✑ ————

During our return journey, I could see that Holmes was still puzzled by certain matters. He would throw off his doubts for a moment, but then his knitted brows would show that the doubts had returned.

Just as our train came to one of the stations near London, Holmes sprang onto the platform, and he pulled me after him. Puzzled, I watched as the last car of the train pulled away.

"Excuse me, my dear fellow," Holmes apologized. "I'm sorry to put you out on a mere whim. But I simply *can't* leave a case in this condition. Every instinct in me cries out against it. The lady's story is complete, and the maid's tale fits in every detail. What do I have to hold up against their stories? Three wine glasses, that's all! Yet if three people truly drank from those glasses, why does each glass not have the usual dregs? Could it be that someone is trying to cover up the real crime?" Holmes's voice rose excitedly as he talked, and I felt my own blood race. This was Holmes at his best.

"Would I," asked Holmes, "have come to different conclusions if I had investigated the dining room in a fresh light, without the women's stories? Yes, of course!

Sit down on the bench, Watson, and listen to the details that excite my suspicions. A return train to Chislehurst Station should be along shortly."

———— ✐ ————

The household at the Abbey Grange was much surprised at our return. Inspector Hopkins had left to send his report to Scotland Yard. So Holmes took over the dining room. He locked the door and devoted himself to a thorough, two-hour-long investigation. I seated myself in a corner and watched his incredible examination as if I were a student and he, the professor.

The window, the drapes, the carpet, the chair, the bellpull—each were checked with the sharpest of eyes. Though the body had been removed, everything else was as it had been. Holmes went from one thing to the next with his magnifying glass. Finally, to my astonishment, he climbed up on the enormous oak mantelpiece.

Far above Holmes's head hung a few inches of red cord. He rested his knee on a wooden brace in the wall and craned his neck toward the ceiling. This brought his hand within just a few inches of the bellpull's dangling end.

At last, he sprang down with a cry of satisfaction. "We have our case, Watson! And it will definitely be one of the most notable in your collection. But how slow-witted I have been! I nearly made the blunder of a lifetime."

"Then you have your men?" I asked, shocked.

"Man, Watson, man—and a most impressive person," Holmes said, pacing. "Strong as a lion—note the blow that bent the poker. Six foot three, limber as a squirrel, and amazingly quick-witted. In the bell rope, we have our answer. Consider this: Where would you expect the bell rope to break? Surely, where it's attached to the wire that leads to the kitchen. Why should it break two inches below that point?"

"Because it was frayed?"

"Not exactly, Watson," explained Holmes. "The man needed the rope. He couldn't tear it down for fear of giving an alarm in the kitchen. So he jumped up on the mantelpiece and placed his knee on the wooden brace. This way, he was able to get within two inches of the ceiling. I figure from this that he is three inches taller than I am. Oh, he was clever! He cut the rope cleanly. But to cover his tracks, he frayed the end he had cut. Thus, it looked as if it had been torn down by the thieves." Holmes rushed to the chair. "And take a look at this, Watson. What do you see?"

"A stain. It looks like dried blood."

"Yes, Watson, my man, blood!" Holmes cried. "The lady lied to us. If she had been sitting in this chair when her husband was murdered, there would be no blood here. I'd wager her black dress has a stain on the bottom of it as well. Now, we must speak with the maid once more. But we must be cunning if we are to get the information we need."

When Holmes approached Theresa Wright, she watched him as if he were a tiger ready to pounce. But eventually my friend's pleasant manner made her relax and speak. She did not even try to conceal her hatred for her late employer.

"Yes, he threw a bottle at me! Sir Eustace was forever ill-treating his wife and me. I'm sure those marks on her arm are from him bruising her. Of course, when he met her, my Miss Mary Fraser of Adelaide, he was all milk and honey. It was in July a year back, for we had just arrived in England. He won her with his title and his money. She was only eighteen and had never been away from home. She made a mistake, that's for sure, but she has paid for it dearly. Do not ask too much of her. She's already gone through more than flesh and blood can stand." With that, Theresa Wright led us back to her mistress.

Lady Brackenstall had returned to the morning room. This time she looked brighter in spirits. But when she saw us enter, she cried out, "Oh, I beg you, do not question me again!"

"Lady Brackenstall," Holmes said gently, "I do not want to make things hard for you. If you will treat me as a friend, I will not betray your trust."

Her eyes opened wide in surprise. "What do you want me to do?"

"Tell the truth."

"Mr. Holmes!"

"No, madam, it is of no use. I would stake all on the fact that your story is a clever work of imagination."

Both mistress and maid stared at Holmes. "Do you mean to say my mistress lied?" stormed the maid.

Holmes turned toward the door and then paused, "Have you nothing to tell then, Lady Brackenstall? Wouldn't it be better to be frank?"

For an instant, the lady of the manor hesitated. Then a mask fell over her face, and she said stonily, "I have told you all I know."

"I'm sorry," Holmes said. He took his hat, and I followed him from the room.

On our way to the abbey gate, we walked past a small pond. A hole was broken in the ice, and a single swan swam around in it. Holmes gazed at the swan, pondering. Then he scribbled a note for the inspector. We presented it to the lodgekeeper for delivery.

"It may be a hit, or it may be a miss," said Holmes lightly, "but we need to make our second visit seem worthwhile. Now, Watson, we're back to London to check the offices of the Adelaide-Southampton Shipping Company. It runs the largest passenger line traveling between South Australia and England."

—— ⌘ ——

When Holmes's card was brought in to the manager of the shipping company, we received instant attention. Holmes asked to see the passenger lists from June and July of 1895. The lists showed that a Miss Mary Fraser and her maid had made a voyage to England on the ship, the *Rock of Gibraltar*. At present, this ship was out to sea with the very same crew. Only the first officer—Mr. Jack Croker—was on shore. Mr. Croker had been made the captain of a new ship, the *Bass Rock*. This ship was due to sail in two days. However, if Holmes cared to wait, he could meet the new captain.

"No," replied Holmes, "but I would be interested in hearing about his record and character."

"There's not an officer in this fleet to touch him," said the manager. "He is completely reliable—although he's a bit hotheaded at times. Still he is loyal, kind, and honest as the day is long."

—— ⌘ ——

Upon leaving the shipping office, we drove to Scotland Yard. But Holmes did not enter. He sat in the cab, lost in thought.

"Are you planning to make a report?" I finally asked.

"No, Watson," he said slowly. "I can't do it. I would rather play tricks with Scotland Yard than with my own conscience. We need to know more to act."

Holmes directed the cabbie to drive to the Charing

Cross Station. There he sent a telegram. Then we made for Baker Street once more.

Before evening, we had an unexpected visit from Inspector Hopkins.

"You must be a wizard, Mr. Holmes," he exclaimed. "How on earth did you know that the silver was at the bottom of the pool?"

"I didn't know it," Holmes replied, lighting his pipe.

"But you told me to look there," objected Hopkins.

"I'm glad to have helped you."

"But you haven't helped me," the inspector fumed, pacing back and forth. "You've made the whole affair more confusing. What reason could the burglars have for throwing their loot into the nearest pond?"

"Perhaps they did not want the silver at all," Holmes responded. "It's possible that the silver was taken to cover up the murder. The silver may have been thrown into the pond simply for a hiding place."

"What a wild idea, Mr. Holmes! But the hiding-place theory suits things," Hopkins said, twisting his hat in his hands. "Even so, I'm a bit weary. I've had a bad setback."

"A setback?" I inquired.

"Yes. The Randall gang was arrested in New York this morning. That takes them off my list of suspects. There are, however, other gangs of three to question, so I must be off."

"You won't stop for supper, then?" asked Holmes. "No? Well, good-bye then. Do let us know how you get on."

The dinner table was cleared before Holmes brought up the subject again. He could see that I was deeply interested in the matter. "My dear fellow," he said, "I expect some intriguing developments in this case quite soon."

"Really? When?"

"From the sounds on the stairs," Holmes answered, "I would say that you shall witness the final act of this remarkable drama within minutes."

Just then, our door opened, and in walked one of the finest-looking men that had ever entered the room. He was tall, golden-mustached, and blue-eyed. The skin on his muscular frame was tanned by tropical suns. He stood with his fists clenched, keeping some powerful emotions in check.

"Sit down, Captain Croker," said Holmes cordially. "You received my telegram?"

Our visitor remained standing. "I got your telegram. Are you going to arrest me? Speak out, man. You can't sit there and play games with me like a cat with a mouse."

"Kindly give the man a cup of tea, Watson," my companion directed. "Sip on that, captain, and calm your nerves. Be frank with me, and we may do some good. Play tricks with me, and I'll crush you."

"What do you wish me to do?" the captain asked suspiciously. He took the tea and slowly seated himself in the armchair I offered.

"Give me the true account of what happened at the Abbey Grange last night," demanded Holmes. "If you go one inch off the straight, I'll blow this police whistle from my window."

The sailor eyed his opponent. Then he slapped his leg. "I'll chance it," he proclaimed. "Right off the top, I regret nothing. But it's the thought that I might bring harm to Mary Fraser that turns my soul to water. . . . You see, Mary and I met on the ship, the *Rock of Gibraltar*. From the first moment I saw her," the captain said with deep emotion, "she was the only woman for me. And I told her so. But she was never engaged to me. Oh, no, she treated me as fairly as ever a woman treated a man. She left the ship free to choose as she would."

Holmes watched the man coolly, giving away nothing.

"The next time we docked, though," the sailor went on, "I heard of her marriage. I was happy for her. I knew she deserved much more than a penniless sailor could give her. But it pained me that I should never see her again. Then one day while I was waiting for orders for my new ship, I caught sight of her maid. The woman drove me half mad with her story. That drunken hound, Sir Eustace—that he should dare to raise a hand against my Mary! Theresa arranged that I could meet Mary on a few occasions. Then my orders arrived. I simply had to see Mary once more before I went back to sea. So last night, I crept up to the house and scratched at the library window. At first, Mary ignored me. But finally she could not leave me out in the frosty night. She whispered for me to come to the dining room so she could let me in.

"As I stood near the window, innocent as a lamb, the beast rushed in like a madman. He called Mary vile names, grabbed her arm, and struck her across the face with his walking stick. I sprang for the poker, and it was a fair fight between us. See—here on my arm is where he struck the first blow. Then it was my turn, and it was all over. It was my life or his!"

Holmes did not comment, and the sailor continued his tale. "Mary had screamed when she was struck, and that brought Theresa down. While Theresa tended to Mary, I opened a bottle of wine and poured a little between Mary's lips. Then I took a drop myself. All the while, Theresa was as cool as ice. It was her plot as well as mine. She kept repeating the story about the burglars to Mary, while I swarmed up and cut the bellpull. Then I tied Mary up and frayed the ends of the cord to make it look natural. Theresa poured a little wine from the two glasses into a third. Then she gathered up the silver for me. On my way out of the garden, I threw the silver into the pond. Theresa and Mary were to wait a quarter of an hour before giving the alarm. And that's the very truth of it, Mr. Holmes."

After the sailor finished speaking, my friend smoked for some time. The captain and I waited in silence. Then Holmes crossed the room and shook our visitor's hand. "I know your words are true. You haven't said one word I didn't already know. The lady must love you deeply for she tried hard to shield you."

Croker smiled slightly. "I thought the police would never see through our dodge."

"The police did not—nor will they, to the best of my belief," said Holmes. "Now, Captain Croker, this is a very serious matter. Yet, if you wish to disappear in the next twenty-four hours, I will not try to stop you."

"And then it will all come out?"

"Most certainly."

The sailor flushed with anger. "What kind of deal is this? I know enough of the law to understand what they will do to Mary. Do you think I would leave her alone to face the music while I slink away? No, sir, do what you want with me, but keep my Mary out of the courts."

"I was only testing you, Captain," said Holmes, with a new tone of respect. He offered our guest his hand once more. "You ring true every time. It's a great responsibility I take upon myself, but I shall not tell the police what I know. I have given Inspector Hopkins an excellent hint, and if he cannot use it, then I can do no more." Holmes took a step backward.

"Stand up, Captain Croker," he commanded. "We'll do this just as the law would. You are the prisoner, and Watson, you are the British jury. I shall be the judge. Gentleman of the jury," declared Holmes in an official tone, "you have heard the evidence. Do you find the prisoner guilty or not guilty?"

"Not guilty, my lord," I said. "It's clear he acted in self-defense."

"Vox populi, vox Dei—the voice of the people is the voice of God." Holmes pounded his fist down onto the table next to him. "You are released, Captain Croker," Holmes pronounced. "As long as the law does not blame another person for this murder, you are safe from me. Come back to this lady in one year, and may your future together prove the wisdom of this night's actions."

From that evening on, the murder of Sir Eustace Brackenstall remained officially unsolved. We heard a rumor a year later that Lady Brackenstall was trying marriage a second time. Her choice of a husband surprised some—for he had no money or title. He was merely the captain of a passenger ship—the *Bass Rock.*

*This case proves that even Sherlock Holmes can be fooled if he believes a conclusion before he gets all the facts. So how did Holmes solve the crime? Check the **CLUES** to find out! See if you were as clever as the master detective.*

CLUES
that led to the solution of
The Adventure of the Abbey Grange

 Holmes's first clue that Lady Brackenstall's story might not be true was the bent poker. The man who killed Sir Eustace had to be very powerful. Could an elderly thief be strong enough to deliver a blow that crushed a man's skull?

 Next, the three wine glasses alerted Holmes to the fact that he needed to investigate further. Only one glass had wine dregs. If all the glasses had been poured at the same time, all three should have had dregs. But they didn't, so Holmes suspected that someone had poured the leftover wine from the first two glasses into the third. The dregs were heavier than the wine, so they slipped more quickly out of the near-empty glasses. This left two glasses with clear wine rings at the bottom and one glass with a ring of dregs. Thus, there were really only two drinkers, and someone was trying to cover things up.

 Other things caught Holmes's attention. Why would the thieves leave a witness to their murder alive? Why would they not finish the bottle of wine? Why didn't they take more than just the silver? Why would they use a bell rope to tie up Lady Brackenstall, when the bell's ringing might alarm the household? All these things seemed suspicious. So Holmes went back for another look.

 The second examination of the dining room showed that the bell rope had been cut rather than yanked down. Only a very tall and limber man could do the job. Since the knots on the bellpull were ones commonly used on ships' ropes, Holmes suspected a sailor.

 Lady Brackenstall had come into contact with sailors a year earlier when she sailed from Australia. So Holmes checked with the shipping company. Only one sailor from her ship—the *Rock of Gibraltar*—had been in England at the time of the murder: Captain Croker. Therefore, Holmes sent the captain a telegram, asking him to visit.

 The fact that the inspector found the missing silver at the bottom of the pond proved Holmes's case. This was not a job of theft. Now Holmes simply had to await the sailor's arrival.

 As Captain Croker entered, Holmes saw that he was tall enough and strong enough to be the murderer. But Holmes knew that Croker was no ordinary murderer because Lady Brackenstall had worked so hard to protect him.

*"He begged the lodgekeeper to come
with him to where his father lay."*

THE BOSCOMBE VALLEY MYSTERY

It had been many months since I had left Baker Street to try married life. One fair June morning, my wife and I were seated at breakfast when the maid brought in a telegram. It was from Sherlock Holmes and ran this way:

> *Have you a couple of days to spare? Was just wired from the west of England about the Boscombe Valley tragedy. Would be glad if you would come with me. Air and scenery perfect. Will leave Paddington Station by the 11:15.*

"Will you go, dear?" asked my wife. "You've been working too hard lately, and a change would do you good. Besides," she added, "you're always so interested in Mr. Holmes's cases."

"I should be ungrateful if I weren't," I replied, "since I met you on one of them." A gentle blush tinted her fresh cheeks. "At any rate," I continued, "you may be right. Dr. Anstruther will surely take care of my patients for a few days." I glanced at my watch. "But if I am to go, I must pack at once."

My army experience in Afghanistan had taught me to pack quickly and lightly. So I was soon in a cab, rattling away to Paddington Station. Sherlock was awaiting me there, pacing up and down the platform. His tall frame looked even thinner and more sharply defined than usual in his gray traveling coat and deer-stalker cloth cap.

"It's so very good of you to come, Watson," said he, shaking my hand.

We boarded the train and found a compartment all to ourselves. Holmes quickly littered it with a pile of newspapers. These he read and reread, taking scrawling notes as he went. "Have you heard anything of the case?" he asked.

"Not a word," I replied. "I haven't seen a paper in some days."

"None of the London newspapers have given the case a full account," Holmes explained. "But from what I have gathered, it seems to be one of those simple cases which are extremely difficult."

"That statement seems strangely at odds with it-self," I remarked.

"Indeed," said Holmes, "but true nonetheless. The more simple and common the crime, the more difficult it is to solve. In this case, a son is accused of killing his father. This may actually be so. But I will take nothing for granted until I've looked into things personally."

Holmes went to the beginning of his notes. "This is how the case stands thus far. Boscombe Valley is a

farm area in Herefordshire. The largest landowner in
the valley is a Mr. John Turner, who made his money
in Australia. One of his properties is Hatherley Farm.
This he rented to a man he had known in Australia,
Charles McCarthy. Turner was the richer man, but he
always treated McCarthy as an equal. These men led
quiet lives, but they were often seen together at hunting and racing occasions. Both men were widowers,
each with one child. Turner has a daughter of about
eighteen, and McCarthy, a son near the same age."

Holmes paused. "Now for the event. Last Monday,
June third, Charles McCarthy told his servant that he
had an appointment to keep at three o'clock. He left his
home close to three and walked down to the Boscombe
Pool. This is a small lake that is halfway between
Hatherley Farm and the Turner estate. McCarthy
never came back from this appointment alive.

"William Crowder, the gamekeeper for Turner's properties, saw McCarthy on his way to the pool. McCarthy
was alone. Within a few minutes, Crowder saw
McCarthy's son, James. The young man had a gun
under his arm and was going the same way. In fact,
Crowder believes that the father was still in sight when
he saw the son. At the time, Crowder thought James
was following his father."

My friend looked up to check that I was paying
attention. Then he continued, "A little while later,
Patricia Moran spotted the father and son together.
Miss Moran is the fourteen-year-old daughter of Turner's lodgekeeper. She was out in the woods picking

spring violets. The father and son were at the edge of
the woods, down by the pool. She heard them shout-
ing at each other. Their argument became heated, and
the son hit his father. This so frightened the girl that
she ran off to tell her mother. The girl had hardly
finished describing the event when James McCarthy
came running up to the lodge. He was screaming that
he had found his father dead. He was extremely upset
and had neither his gun nor his hat. Fresh blood
stained his right hand and sleeve. He begged the
lodgekeeper to come with him to where his father lay.

"The lodgekeeper found the body stretched out in
the grass next to the pool. The head had been struck
by a blunt weapon. The wound could have been made
by the end of the son's rifle, but it had no blood on it.
The gun was found in the grass only a few paces from
the body. James McCarthy was later arrested and
charged with the murder of his father."

"I see," said I. "I could hardly imagine a more
hopeless case for the boy. All the circumstances point
to him."

"True," Holmes agreed. "But evidence of this type
can be a tricky thing. If one approaches the evidence
from a different direction, it suddenly points just as
straight to the opposite conclusion. For example, young
James did not seem the least bit surprised to be arrested. He commented that it was certainly no more
than he deserved."

I jumped on this. "There we have a confession!
That alone should prove his guilt, should it not?"

"Not at all, Watson," stated Holmes. "Immediately after saying these things, McCarthy declared his innocence. He would have to have been a fool, indeed, not to have seen the case against him. If he had acted surprised or outraged, I would have trusted him less. But McCarthy covered up nothing. And he seemed to feel a great guilt for having argued with his father. These actions seem to me to be signs of a healthy and entirely innocent mind."

"Maybe so, Holmes," I replied. "But many men have been hanged on far less evidence."

"Yes," Holmes nodded thoughtfully. "And many men have been wrongfully hanged. There is nothing more misleading than an obvious fact."

"Does McCarthy's own story shed any hope on his case?" I asked.

"I'm afraid it is not very encouraging, Watson," said Holmes. He tossed me the Herefordshire paper. "Take a look for yourself."

The local paper had devoted a long section to the initial investigation. It read:

Examiner: In your own words, tell us what you know of this tragedy.
McCarthy: I had been away in Bristol for three days. When I returned early Monday afternoon, my father was in town. Some time later, I glanced out the window of the house and saw his carriage arrive. He got out and began walking rapidly away from the house. I had no idea where he was

heading. Since my father was obviously busy, I decided to hunt some rabbits down in the glen near the pool. I left the window to fetch my gun.

On my way to the glen, I saw Mr. Crowder. But he is mistaken in his belief that I was following my father. He was not within my sight. When I was about a hundred yards from the pool, I heard someone call out "Coooee!" This is a call they use in Australia, and it was a signal between my father and me. I hurried to the pool, where he was standing. He seemed surprised to see me. He asked me what I thought I was doing there. We got into an argument, and it came to blows. As many know, my father had a violent temper.

I was so angry, I stomped off. I was not more than a hundred and fifty yards away when I heard a hideous cry of pain and came running back. My father was on the ground, bleeding terribly. I dropped my gun and picked him up in my arms. He soon died. I held him for a few minutes and then ran to the lodgekeeper's for help. I don't know how he came to be wounded. Mr. Crowder was the only person I had seen in the area. Unfortunately, my father was not a well-liked man. He had had arguments with almost everyone who knew him. But I don't know of anyone who would have done him in.

Examiner: *Why did you and your father quarrel?*
McCarthy: *I would prefer not to answer that. It had nothing to do with what happened.*
Examiner: *That is for us to decide. I am afraid*

you have no choice but to answer.

McCarthy: *I must refuse.*

Examiner: *This shall not go well with you. Now, if your father did not know you were near, why should he yell the signal "Coooee"?*

McCarthy: *I do not know. (This was said with much confusion.)*

Examiner: *When you found your father wounded, did you see anything suspicious?*

McCarthy: *Not exactly. I seem to remember something lying on the ground near him, a cloak perhaps. I think it was gray, maybe a plaid of some sort. However, when I got up from my father and looked around for it, it was gone.*

Examiner: *Where was it lying exactly?*

McCarthy: *As near as I can recall, it was maybe a dozen yards away, halfway between my father and the edge of the woods.*

Examiner: *And you say it was removed somehow while you were holding your father?*

McCarthy: *Yes. My back was turned, and I was only paying attention to my father.*

Examiner: *Did your father say anything before he died?*

McCarthy: *No. He seemed delirious, mumbling something about a rat. But it made no sense at all to me.*

Examiner: *This concludes our examination of the witness.*

I folded up the newspaper. "It seems, Holmes, that

the examiner clearly noted the most important points. McCarthy must be hiding something! He won't explain the quarrel, and he says that his father signaled him— yet McCarthy didn't know his son was near."

Holmes laughed softly to himself and stretched out upon the cushioned seat. "Ah, my dear Watson," said he, "both you and the examiner point out those items that are strongest in the boy's favor. If he were truly guilty, wouldn't he have come up with a better story than that?" My companion smiled and pulled out a book of Italian poetry, which he read silently until we arrived at the station.

It was nearly four o'clock when we finally found ourselves in the pretty little country town of Ross. As we stepped off the train, a lean, weasel-faced man approached us. Even in uniform, Inspector Lestrade of Scotland Yard had a sly, undercover look. He shook our hands and then led us down the street to our rooms at the Hereford Arms Inn.

"It seems a shame, Mr. Holmes," said the inspector as we were unpacking, "to have dragged you into the country for a case as simple as this. The more you go into it, the plainer it becomes. But one can't refuse a lady. Turner's daughter, Alice, had heard of you. It was she who insisted your opinion was necessary. I told her repeatedly that there is nothing you can do that I have not already done."

Glancing out the window, Lestrade added, "Why, bless my soul, that's her carriage in front of the inn."

He had hardly spoken when a lovely young woman burst into the room. She talked excitedly, her violet eyes shining.

"Oh, Mr. Sherlock Holmes!" she cried, immediately picking out my companion. "I am Alice Turner, and I am so glad that you have come. I know James didn't do it, and I know you can prove it! I grew up with James, and he is too tenderhearted to swat a fly."

"I hope we may clear him," said Holmes, rising to greet her. "I shall do all I can."

"See there," she said triumphantly, glaring at Lestrade. "He gives me hope."

The inspector shrugged. "I'm afraid Mr. Holmes may have been a little hasty in his conclusions."

"But he is right!" she said. "I'm sure, Mr. Holmes, that James and his father were quarreling about me. That is why James would not explain the argument. He did not want to draw me into the case. His father kept pushing James to marry me, but James felt we were too young. He wanted to see something of the world first."

Holmes's eyes took on the familiar glint of interest. "Was your father in favor of such a marriage?"

"No," she answered. "He was strongly against it. Mr. McCarthy was the only one hoping for the marriage." Holmes shot one of his keen, questioning glances at her, and Miss Turner blushed.

"Thank you for this information," said Holmes. "May I call on your father tomorrow?"

"Oh, no, Mr. Holmes. The doctor wouldn't allow it. Haven't you heard? Poor father has been ailing for some time, and this has broken him down completely. Mr. McCarthy was the only man who knew my father from the old days."

"In Australia?"

"Yes," she answered. "From the gold mines there. That is how my father made his money. Now, I must go back to him. But, Mr. Holmes, if you see James, please tell him that I know he is innocent."

"I will deliver your message, Miss Turner."

With that assurance, the young woman left as swiftly as she had come. Meanwhile, Lestrade was shaking his head. Finally he spoke up. "I'm ashamed of you, Mr. Holmes. You're raising the girl's hopes only to crush them. I'm not soft of heart, but I call that cruel."

"I am confident, Inspector, that I shall be able to clear him," Holmes stated. "May we see the prisoner yet this evening?"

"Yes." Lestrade looked unconvinced that Holmes's

work would lead to anything. "I have permission for the two of us."

"Then let us go," said Holmes. "You might find it a bit dull for a while, Watson. But I shall be back within a couple of hours."

After they left, I tried to interest myself in a novel. But the plot seemed flat compared to the real-life story of James McCarthy. So I picked up the local paper Holmes had left. It gave a description of the injury found on McCarthy's head. From the medical information, I pieced together that McCarthy must have been struck from behind and from the left.

I could go no further on my own, so I waited for Sherlock to return.

———— ✑ ————

Late was the hour when Holmes finally came back. He tossed off his cap and coat, and sat down on a chair near the window.

"Well, Watson," he said sighing, "that visit was rather disappointing. I had hoped that young McCarthy might have some clue about his father's murderer. But I'm convinced he is as puzzled as everyone else. He seems a good-hearted lad, though, and one that ladies would call fine looking."

"He may be," said I. "But he certainly has no taste in women if he doesn't find Miss Turner appealing."

"Ah, my dear fellow," said Holmes, "a painful tale hangs on that. Contrary to what we've heard, the young man is madly, insanely in love with the girl.

Unfortunately, when he was but sixteen, he fell into a fancy over a maid down in Bristol. This was before Miss Turner had returned from boarding school. James married the girl in secret.

"Now mark this point, Watson," Holmes directed. "James's father never knew about his son's visits to the wife in Bristol. When the two met in the woods, James's father yelled at him for not proposing to Miss Turner. This sent the youth into a frenzy. That is why the argument came to blows."

"Oh, the boy is in a bit of a rub," I said, feeling sorry for him.

"Yes, but some good has come out of it all," said Holmes. "When the girl in Bristol read about James's arrest, she got scared. She wrote James a letter confessing that she already had a husband in Bermuda. Therefore, his marriage is illegal, and James is now quite free to marry whomever he would choose."

"I suppose that makes him feel a little better."

"Some," Holmes agreed solemnly. "I was able to uncover a few other loose ends as well. It seems that Crowder, Turner's gamekeeper, often got into arguments with the elder McCarthy over hunting rights on Turner properties. No one recalls seeing Crowder after the murder. James, however, could not remember the color of the coat Crowder was wearing when he spotted him in the woods."

Holmes looked thoughtful. "Tomorrow we'll investigate the scene of the murder. Then maybe we can give the boy some real reason to hope."

At nine o'clock the next morning, Lestrade called for us in a carriage. We set straight off for Hatherley Farm and the Boscombe Pool.

On the way, Lestrade filled us in on the latest news. "Mr. Turner has taken a turn for the worse. His daughter fears he shall not live long."

"What is the source of his illness?" I inquired.

"It must be the shock of McCarthy's death," Lestrade replied. "They were quite close. Turner even gave Hatherley Farm to McCarthy free of rent."

"Indeed!" said Holmes. "That is interesting. Is it not strange that the penniless McCarthy was pushing for a marriage of his son to Turner's daughter when he knew Turner was against it?"

"It doesn't seem that unusual," said Lestrade. Then winking at me, he added, "I have a hard enough time dealing with the facts, Mr. Holmes, without flying away after theories and fancies."

"You are right, Inspector," said Holmes politely. "You do have difficulty tackling the facts."

"Well, I can see one fact clearly enough," snapped Lestrade. "The boy killed his father—probably in an argument over the girl. All the rest is moonshine."

"Maybe so, but moonshine is brighter than fog," said Holmes, laughing. "Now, if I'm not mistaken, that's Hatherley Farm on our left."

The old stone house spread out comfortably, with two stories and a slate roof. A maid answered the door. At Holmes's request, she brought him the boots of her dead master, as well as those of his son. Holmes measured each boot from some seven or eight points.

Then Holmes noticed a map of Australia on the wall. The maid smiled and pointed to the colony of Victoria and the hills around Ballarat. "This is where Mr. Mc-Carthy worked in the gold mines," she explained.

"Had Mr. McCarthy received any letters or visitors from Victoria recently?" Holmes asked.

"No, sir," the maid said, lowering her eyes. "He did not have many friends."

"I see. That will be enough for now," said Holmes.

———— ∽ ————

After leaving Hatherley Farm, we took the winding trail that led to the Boscombe Pool. The woods around us were quiet, since they were closed to outsiders. The grounds could only be reached from Hatherley Farm or the Turner estate.

We came to the pool, and Sherlock Holmes went to work. When he was hot upon a scent such as this, he was transformed. Those who knew Holmes only as the quiet reasoner would not have recognized him now. His brow tightened into two dark lines, and his eyes shone with a steely glitter. Like a dog hard on a chase, he went swiftly and silently along a track in the grass. He traveled up and down the marshy meadow with his back bent over and his spyglass at his eye. At any moment, he would suddenly sprawl on the ground for a closer look.

As he worked, he began to mutter to himself. "Yes, these are the youth's feet . . . twice he was walking . . . once he ran . . . his toe marks are strongly indented . . . here, yes, here are his father's boots . . . the place where he lay . . . the butt end of the rifle rested here as the boy listened to his father . . . my goodness, Inspector, that left foot of yours, with its inward twist, is all over everything! A mole could trace it . . . I would have been more fortunate to have buffalo wallow through . . . Ah, ha! This is it! The square toes, most unusual, they come and go . . . they come again . . . long lengths between each print . . . tiptoe, yes, on tiptoe . . . he leans more heavily on the left. Indeed, the gray cloak! He must have returned for the cloak. This proves it . . ."

Back and forth, Holmes worked, eventually stopping at the base of a tree. It lay some yards from the scene, near the edge of the woods. In the moss around the roots, he discovered the butt of a small cigar and some ashes. He passed them to me for inspection. The unsmoked end of the cigar had been bluntly cut and had not been bitten.

Holmes moved on to examine a large, jagged stone. He had found it lying on the grass near one of the tree roots. Finally he rose and handed the stone to the impatient Lestrade.

"Inspector," said Holmes, "you may file this as evidence. It is the murder weapon."

"You must be joking, Mr. Holmes. There is not a mark upon it," Lestrade replied.

"Since there was grass growing under the stone," my companion explained, "it is obvious that the object has been laying here only a few days. The stone matches the wound, and no definite weapon has yet been found."

"And I suppose you know the murderer as well," Lestrade said sarcastically.

"He is a tall man, left-handed, who limps with the right leg. He wears thick-soled, square-toed boots and a gray cloak. He smokes Indian cigars, uses a cigar holder, and carries a blunt penknife in his pocket. There are other things as well, but this should be enough to aid our search."

As usual, I was taken by surprise at the amount of information Holmes had discovered. Lestrade, however, laughed aloud. "My dear Mr. Holmes," said the inspector, grinning, "your theories are all well and good, but I am hardly going to stride about the neighborhood looking for a tall, left-handed man with a game foot. I'd be the laughingstock of Scotland Yard. Until we have more proof than a few blades of grass, I will have to solve this case my own way."

"Quite right," said Holmes. "I have given you a chance. Now I must go about my business. I'll be busy this afternoon, but we shall leave by this evening. The case will be solved by then."

The inspector snickered in disbelief, but said nothing more. Holmes left us in the carriage and made a quick detour on foot to the lodgekeeper's house to leave a message.